MOONBEAR'S SHADOW

A MOONBEAR Book

• FRANK ASCH •

ALADDIN
NEW YORK   LONDON   TORONTO   SYDNEY   NEW DELHI

ALADDIN

An imprint of Simon & Schuster Children's Publishing Division

1230 Avenue of the Americas, New York, NY 10020

This Aladdin edition August 2014

For information about special discounts for bulk purchases, please contact

Simon & Schuster Special Sales at 1-866-506-1949 or business@simonandschuster.com.

The Simon & Schuster Speakers Bureau can bring authors to your live event.

For more information or to book an event contact the Simon & Schuster Speakers Bureau

at 1-866-248-3049 or visit our website at www.simonspeakers.com.

Designed by Karina Granda

The text of this book was set in Olympian LT Std.

Manufactured in China 0915 SCP

10 9 8 7 6 5 4 3

Library of Congress Cataloging-in-Publication Data

Asch, Frank

Bear Shadow

Summary: Bear tries everything he can think of to get rid of his shadow.

Children's stories, American. [1. Bears—Fiction. 2. Shadows—Fiction] I. Title.

PZ7.A778Be 1984

[E] 84-18250

ISBN 978-1-4424-9427-5 (hc)

ISBN 978-1-4424-9426-8 (pbk)

ISBN 978-1-4424-9428-2 (eBook)

To Devin

One day Bear went down to the pond with his fishing pole and a big can of worms. While he was putting a worm on his hook, he looked down and saw a big fish.

I'm going to catch that fish, thought Bear to himself.

But when Bear stood up to throw his line in the water, his shadow scared the big fish away.

"Go away, Shadow!" cried Bear.

But Bear's shadow would not go away.

"Okay," said Bear. "If you won't go on your own, then I'll just have to get rid of you!" And he put down his fishing pole and began to run.

He ran around the pond. When he got to the other side, he kept on running.

He ran through a field of flowers, jumped over the brook and hid behind a tree.

Good! thought Bear. *Now Shadow can't find me!*

But Bear was wrong.

When he stepped out from behind the tree, the first thing he saw was Shadow.

Nearby was a cliff. Bear walked over to the cliff and looked up.

I'll climb so high Shadow won't be able to follow me, thought Bear.

Bear climbed higher and higher until at last he pulled himself up to the top.

Huffing and puffing, he smiled with pride.

Then he looked down and saw Shadow.

Now Bear was very annoyed, so he went home and got a hammer and some nails to nail his shadow to the ground.

He hammered and hammered and hammered, but no matter how many nails he hammered, he couldn't nail his shadow down.

If I can't nail him down, thought Bear, *maybe I can bury him.*

So he got his shovel and dug a hole. When the hole was deep and wide, he let his shadow fall in the hole.

Then Bear filled in the hole with dirt. When he was finished, it was almost noon.

The sun was high in the sky and Shadow was nowhere to be seen.

"At last!" sighed Bear. "No more shadow!"

But now Bear was very tired.

So he went inside and took a little nap.

While he slept, time passed and the sun

once again cast shadows everywhere.

When Bear got up and opened his door, he saw his shadow on the floor.

"Not you again!" exclaimed Bear. And he slammed the door, hoping to lock Shadow inside. But Shadow was too quick.

"Mmm," sighed Bear, "How about this . . . If you let me catch a fish, I'll let you catch one too. Nod your head like this if it's a deal."

When Bear nodded his head, Shadow nodded too.

So Bear went back to the pond and once again threw his line in the water.

By this time the sun was in a different part of the sky, which made it easy for Shadow to keep his part of the deal.

And when Bear caught that big fish,

Shadow caught one too.